THE FRANKENSTEIN JOURNALS

Written by Scott Sonneborn

D0673439

Raintree is an imprint of Capstone Global Library Limited, a company incorporated in England and Wales having its registered office at 7 Pilgrim Street, London, EC4V 6LB – Registered company number: 6695582

www.raintree.co.uk
myorders@raintree.co.uk

Text and illustrations © Capstone Global Library Limited 2016
The moral rights of the proprietor have been asserted.

All rights reserved. No part of this publication may be reproduced in any form or by any means (including photocopying or storing it in any medium by electronic means and whether or not transiently or incidentally to some other use of this publication) without the written permission of the copyright owner, except in accordance with the provisions of the Copyright, Designs and Patents Act 1988 or under the terms of a licence issued by the Copyright Licensing Agency, Saffron House, 6–10 Kirby Street, London EC1N 8TS (www.cla.co.uk). Applications for the copyright owner's written permission should be addressed to the publisher.

Printed and bound in China

ISBN 978 1 4747 0743 5

CITY AND COUNTY OF SWANSEA LIBRARIES	
6000252524	
Askews & Holts	10-Nov-2015
	£5.99
BR	

…e British Library.

…rs of material reproduced in
…printings if notice is given to

A Pain in the Butt

Chapter 1

Hey, so, hello, my future self!

Seeing as you've probably already read the previous chapters in my journal, you should know the story: I wrote all this stuff down in my journal so you would always remember how you met all of our cousins.

I suppose there's a chance parts of my journal might have been lost. Or stolen. Or maybe your mind got wiped fighting in the robot wars or whatever it is people are doing thirty years from now.

In that case, here's what you need to know:

I grew up in an orphanage. No one knew who had left me there, or what my name was. So Mr Shelley, the head of the orphanage, called me John Doe.

JD for short.

Growing up in the orphanage, the one thing I wanted was a big family. And then one day I found Dr Victor Von Frankenstein's journal. In it, he revealed all the secrets about how he created his monster.

The journal also held an even bigger secret (at least to me). I was the son of...

FRANKENSTEIN'S MONSTER!

I have to admit it was a shock to find out I was the son of a famous monster. Mostly because it meant I had a HUGE family!

Think about it. I inherited all my mismatched arms and hands and ears from my dad.

The way I thought about it, the people he got those body parts from were my relatives. I have their legs, feet and eyes, the same way other kids have their grandmother's ears or their great-uncle's nose.

Of course, those people were probably all dead. (At least, I hoped they were dead before Dr Frankenstein took parts from their bodies and put them in my dad!)

But those people probably had children and grandchildren. They would be related to me too – they'd be like my cousins!

All I had to do was find out who they were. The clues I needed were all in Dr Frankenstein's journal. And as I already mentioned, I had found Dr F's journal, so that should have been a piece of cake, right?

Wrong.

Dr Frankenstein's daughter Fran Kenstein stole the journal from me. The only thing I had now were copies of just a few of the pages.

Fran also wanted to find my cousins – to use them to make a new monster.

And by "use them", I mean chop them up and take their body parts! So I had to find them first.

I had already found three: Robert, Sam and Gloria.

Gloria was the Vampire's bodyguard. That's a job that took a lot of guts.

I had the same sort of guts Gloria did. That's how we were related: through my dad's large intestine.

That didn't mean I was as brave as Gloria, but I did my best when we ran into the Invisible Man and – well, that's a whole other story (Literally! Check out other parts of my journal, if you don't remember).

All you need to know now is that I helped Gloria to protect the Vampire from the Invisible Man.

The Vampire was grateful. He was also immortal. That meant he'd probably live forever.

You know how old people tend to collect a lot of stuff over the years? Well, the Vampire was hundreds of years old. He had a load of old stuff.

WOOOOO!

Including a stash of gold coins.

He gave me a few to say "thank you".

Gloria still had her job to do, protecting the Vampire while he slept through the days in his retirement home in Florida.

But with the gold coins he had given me, I had more than enough money to go anywhere in the world to meet the rest of my cousins.

Now I just had to work out where to go.

Before Fran did!

DUN DUN DUN...

Chapter 2

I knew the clues I needed to find all of my cousins were in the pages of Dr Frankenstein's journal. Unfortunately, I didn't have all the pages. And the ones I had were all jumbled up and out of order.

What I needed was someone who could help me work them out. Someone who knew all about Dr Frankenstein and would be able to help me fill in what I was missing.

Of course, I had already met someone like that: Fran. But there was no way she was going to help me.

So I searched the internet for other people who knew about Dr F and his monster. And I found some. Most of them worked at the Department of Monster Studies at the Main Branch of the New York Public Library in Manhattan.

I had plenty of money, so that's where I went.

As I walked past the stone lions that guarded the library steps, I was nervous. Up until now, I had needed to work out everything on my own. Inside, would I finally find someone who could help me to track down my cousins? And maybe even my dad?

Nope. Turned out that, due to budget cuts, the Department of Monster Studies was only open from midday until four. On Tuesdays. It was Wednesday. I was on my own again (at least until next Tuesday).

I found an empty table and took out my journal. I spread out all the pages I had from Dr F's journal.

I didn't have all of Dr F's journal. That made it difficult to understand what was written on the pages I did have.

What made it even more difficult was that the pages seemed to be out of order. Like this one. It said "The End", but it was in the middle of the pages I had.

The End.

Another page said "Thanks to Princeton University", which I thought was maybe because Dr F went there or something. You know, as though he was thanking them for teaching him all the things he wrote about doing in his journal.

But as I spread all the pages I had from his journal out on the big wooden table, I saw something else.

Underneath "The End" there was a stain. Maybe it was from Dr Frankenstein's coffee? Or lunch?

That didn't matter. What did matter was that it was only half a stain. Like half of the lunch (or coffee) had fallen on this page and half on another page.

I rifled through the pages I had. And then I found it! The stains matched! "The End" didn't mean the end of the book. It meant the end, as in REAR END. In other words, the butt! HAHAHAHA!

I had a clue! Frankenstein hadn't written "Thanks to Princeton University" to say thank you for his education.

Acquired 8.07 pm. 26 Sept.

width 60cm

45cm height

TOP SECRET

22kg weight

Somehow, Dr F had got my dad's butt thanks to Princeton University.

I ran to the library's computer room, sat down and quickly typed in "Princeton" and "Rear End". I made sure to search just for news articles and not images.

After scrolling through several pages of results, I finally found what I was looking for.

Bertram Wodehouse III.

He had gone to Princeton. As had his father and grandfather. Like them, Bertram III had donated a lot of money to the university when he died.

Unlike them, he had also donated his body! His body was given to the biology department so they could use it for "the advancement of science".

But before they could advance any science, the body was stolen! There were a load of articles about that. The robbery had taken place at 8.07 p.m. on 26 September.

The same date and time as in Dr F's journal!

I read the rest of the articles. The police never discovered who stole the body. But I knew who had: Dr Frankenstein. He had taken Bertram III's butt and given it to my dad!

Bertram III was already dead when that happened. But the articles about him also mentioned that he had a son, Bertram IV.

I read online that Bertram IV went to Princeton University, like his dad and grandad and great-grandad. But that was pretty much all I found. I tried to look up a phone number or email address for Bertram and came up with nothing. And the only thing I could find about what he had done after university was that he was now a member of the Princeton Club in New York.

Wait! The Princeton Club in New York! New York! That's where I was!

I searched online and found the address of the Princeton Club. It was just around the corner from the library!

EXCELLENT!

A couple of minutes later, I spun through the revolving door of the Princeton Club.

"May I help you?" asked a woman behind the desk in a very quiet voice.

I told her I was looking for Bertram Wodehouse.

"He's in the lounge," she replied as quietly as before. "But I'm afraid our club policy is quite strict. The lounge is a quiet zone."

"Which means," she said in a soft voice, "anything above a whisper will not be tolerated."

She pointed to a table at the back of the lounge.

"Bertram is over there," she whispered. "And do keep your voice down."

I saw a man wider than he was tall. He was wearing a jacket and tie and sitting in a very comfy-looking chair having coffee. With Fran Kenstein!!!!

Chapter 3

I didn't know what to do. Should I run? Try to sneak up on Fran and tackle her?

Don't panic, I told myself. *You'll work something out.* But I didn't get the chance to work anything out. Because Fran waved me over to their table!

She turned and whispered something to Bertram. He nodded and waved me over too!

I couldn't just leave my cousin with Fran. So I marched over there. As Bertram sipped his coffee, Fran ate some guacamole.

She ate it without crisps. Or a spoon. Which didn't look easy. But Fran never did things the easy way.

Whatever Fran was plotting to do to Bertram, she hadn't done it yet. That meant I still had time to warn him.

But I couldn't just tell him we were related through my dad's butt. What were the odds he'd believe that? And if he didn't believe me, he wouldn't listen to my warnings.

I had to be clever. I couldn't tell him too much too soon and risk freaking him out. So I started slowly. "Hi, Bertram," I said. "My name's JD."

"Hello there," replied Bertram as I sat down at his table. "Do I know you? You look a bit … peculiar."

I get that a lot — mostly because I've got one green eye and one blue one. And one of my hands is bigger than the other. And one of my legs is shorter than the other.

"JD gets his looks from his dad," Fran said.

"Don't listen to her," I told Bertram. "I mean, yes, I do get my looks from my dad. She's right about that. But she's the reason I'm here to see you. I would've called or emailed, but I couldn't find your number or email address."

"Oh, I don't use email," he replied. "Or have a telephone. I thought about getting one once, but buying it seemed like too much  trouble. I mean, you have to go to the shops. Can you imagine that? Going all the way to a shop?!" he said.

That didn't sound like a lot of work to me, but I didn't want to be rude. So I agreed with him. "I suppose when you put it like that, it does sound tough," I said. "It's just that if you had had a phone, it would have been a lot easier to get in touch with you."

"Easier for you, perhaps," he replied with a smile. "But not for me. If I had had a phone, I would have had to pick it up and probably press some buttons and whatnot to answer it. But as I don't have one, all I had to do is sit here with this nice young woman, while you arrived to tell me whatever it is you want to tell me."

"Well, what I wanted to tell you is that this young woman isn't nice at all!" I exclaimed. "You've got to get out of here, Bertram!"

"SHHH!" hushed several club members.

"Sorry!" I whispered back.

"You shouldn't do that," said Fran.

"What? Talk loudly?" I replied. "Or try to save Bertram?"

"No," she said. "I meant you shouldn't call him Bertram. He prefers Bertie."

"Yes, please call me Bertie," said my cousin. "As I told the young lady, 'Bertram' is such a bother to say."

Chapter 4

"I do not have to believe you," he said. "In fact, it would be far better for me if I did not. Because if I believed what you said, JD, it would ruin this perfectly pleasant coffee I'm having and require me to get up and do something."

"And there's nothing that's more of a bother than doing something," added Bertie. "I've spent my whole life avoiding it."

Fran just sat there smiling. It began to dawn on me why she hadn't done anything yet. Because she didn't have to. She had all the time in the world.

It didn't seem as though Bertie was going anywhere. And seeing as he weighed more than twice as much as me, there was no way I could make him move.

I had to convince him.

"Okay, I know this is a little hard to believe," I told Bertie. "But my dad was Frankenstein's Monster. And he got his, well, rear end from your dad. And I inherited my bottom from him. Which means we're related through our butts!"

Bertie shook his head. "I simply refuse to believe it."

"I know it's a little hard to swallow," I admitted. "But it's the truth." I told him about my other cousins and how I had found them through my dad's feet, eye and guts.

"Oh, no, you misunderstand," said Bertie. "I don't find it preposterous that we are related through our posteriors."

"And I have no trouble at all believing in monsters," he went on. "After all, one of my best friends at the club is one. Isn't that right, Tutty?"

Bertie waved over to the next table. It was only then that I saw that the person at the next table wasn't a person at all. It was the Mummy!

Boy, did that mummy stink! I mean, he smelled awful. He probably hadn't changed his bandages in over 3,000 years.

But he also stunk as a person. A couple of years ago, he made a huge mess in my hometown. Some people said it had all been a misunderstanding. Which I suppose made sense – it was impossible to understand his moans and groans. But no one from Victorville would ever be happy to see this mummy.

Of course, Bertie wasn't from Victorville. He waved cheerfully at the Mummy.

"UNHHHH!" groaned the Mummy as he waved back at Bertie.

"SHHHHH!" whispered the club members at a nearby table.

I knew they didn't like it when people raised their voices in here. I suppose they didn't like it when mummies did it either.

Bertie turned to me. "So I have no difficulty in believing that it's quite possible my father's rear end could have gone into Frankenstein's Monster. And that that monster is your father."

"Great! Then you know we're related!" I exclaimed.

"SHHH!!!" hushed the people around us.

"I do not believe we are related at all," Bertie whispered to me. "How could I be related to someone like you through my father's posterior? After all, my father sat on that rear end in this very same club I am a member of now, doing nothing for his whole life. Just as my grandfather did. And just as I'm doing now."

Bertie pointed over his shoulder. Hanging on the wall above him were framed paintings of his father and grandfather. They were sitting in the club in the very same chair Bertie was sitting in now.

"For generations," said Bertie, "my family has done nothing. Zero. Zilch," he told me. "What I'm saying is: you told me you have raced all around the world chasing after your cousins, correct?"

I nodded. That was true.

"Well, it exhausts me just to think about having such an adventure," said Bertie. "My goal in life is to have no goals in life. Just like my father and my grandfather. You are simply nothing like my family."

"And that," Bertie continued, "means we can't be related. Which means I'm not in any danger from Ms Kenstein here. Which is wonderful. Because if I were in danger, I'd have to do something about it. And that would interfere with my routine."

"I always follow the same routine every day," said Bertie. "After all, trying to think of something new to do every day is an awful lot of work. Sticking to my routine allows me to avoid all that bother."

"You always do the exact same thing every day?" Fran asked pointedly.

"Absolutely," beamed Bertie. Then, his face darkened. "Well, except for one day. The eighteenth of March. Seven years ago. I did something very different that day."

"What?" I asked.

"I skipped my midday coffee at the club! It was a disaster!" he shuddered. "I will never stray from my routine like that again!"

He looked at his watch. "In which case, I need to get going," he said.

Bertie got up and started to leave.

I looked at Fran. I expected her to tackle him and grab his butt. Maybe not grab it. But, well, you know what I mean.

9AM–
Try AND WAKE UP

10 AM–
Actually WAKE UP

12 PM–
coffee at the Princeton Club

2PM–
Return to room at the St Regis Hotel to Read the newspaper

4PM–
Tea at the Rainbow Room

6PM–
Dinner at the Club

7PM–
Coffee at the St Regis Hotel

8PM–
Go to bed

But Fran just sat there smiling as Bertie walked away.

Instead of doing anything about his butt, she just sat on hers and said to me, "So, here we are."

Yeah, I thought, here I am with a crazy person who wants to chop up my cousins to build a new monster! And it's not as though she has any nicer plans for me!

So then why was she just letting Bertie walk away?

"It's not often we find ourselves sitting together in a nice place like this, is it?" she asked.

That was true. Mostly because every time we met, Fran did things like try to get me arrested or light the air around me on fire with an air fryer!

Wait – was that why she let Bertie go? Because she wanted to take care of me first? Fran leaned in and whispered, "You've kept me from three of your cousins so far. This time, I will stop at nothing to get my hands on Bertie's butt."

"Then why'd you let him go?" I shouted.

"SHH!!" hushed the club members.

"I didn't," whispered Fran. "He's with my associate now."

I looked over and saw Bertie getting his coat from the cloakroom. Then he headed to the door.

"I don't see anyone with him," I whispered back.

"Of course you don't!" gloated Fran, a little too loudly for the other club members. "SHH!" they all hushed her.

Fran scowled. Then she scribbled something on a napkin and slid it over to me.

I read Fran's note.

"You mean, my dad!?!" I exclaimed loudly.

"Shh!" said the club members again.

"I've never seen him because I never got to meet him!" I whispered to Fran. "Do you know where he is?!"

"Well, actually, I –" started Fran. Then she stopped and said, "That's a story for another time. My note wasn't about your father. Think again. Who is someone you've met that you've never seen?"

"How could I meet someone without seeing them?" I asked. "I mean, they'd have to be invisible or –"

Oh, no!

I knew who Fran meant.

THE INVISIBLE MAN!

"I can see you know who I mean." Fran smiled. "Given what happened the last time you met him, the Invisible Man has given up on getting revenge on the Vampire."

Okay, well, that's good, I thought.

"Now he wants revenge on YOU!" said Fran.

"That's why he's helping me," said Fran. "I thought you'd show up and try to interfere again. I am very clever, after all."

OH NO!

Chapter 5

"So I told the Invisible Man that if he worked for me, he was bound to run into you," Fran went on. "All I asked for in exchange is that he grab Bertram first. That's why I was happy to sit here, doing nothing. I was waiting for Bertram to get outside where the Invisible Man is waiting to grab him!"

It looked like that was about to happen. Well, okay, it didn't look like that. All I could see was Bertie putting his coat on and walking out through the club's revolving door.

But I knew the Invisible Man had to be somewhere just outside.

There was no way I could run all the way across the club in time. And even if I could, what would I do then? Tackle the Invisible Man? How? I couldn't even see him.

But he could hear me.

"Hey! Invisible Man!" I shouted.

"Shhh!!!" hushed the club members around me.

"I'm right here!" I shouted. "I'm the one you want!"

All the club members looked at me like I was crazy. Including Bertie. And the Mummy, who GROAAAANED.

But it worked! Suddenly, the revolving door to the club spun. Then one table, and then another, tipped over and fell to the floor.

The Invisible Man was knocking them over as he made his way to me! Of course, Bertie didn't know that was what was happening. So he turned and walked out into the street. He was safe!

But I wasn't!

"No!" Fran shouted at the Invisible Man as he ran towards me. "What are you doing? Go back and get Bertram before he gets away!"

"SHH!" a club member shouted back at her.

"Oh, will you be quiet?" said an exasperated Fran.

"Will YOU?" replied the club member.

Fran scowled and turned back to my chair. Which was empty! While she had been distracted by the club member, I had taken off running.

I didn't know if I could make it past the Invisible Man to the front door. So I took off in the opposite direction, hoping there was another way out.

Napkins and glasses flew off tables behind me. The Invisible Man was chasing after me! Which meant he wasn't chasing Bertie. That was good. But if he caught me, that would be bad. Very bad!

I ran through a door and into the kitchen. I ran past fryers or grills or whatever you call those things that cook food.

At the very end of the kitchen, I found a door and burst through it.

Outside, I found myself in an alley and stopped to take a deep breath of New York City air. It smelled like a mixture of rubbish and cat wee.

"Oh, this is too disgusting!" said a voice.

I turned back and saw a piece of chewing gum stretch up from the pavement into the air.

It took me a second, but then I realized the Invisible Man must have stepped in that gum and now it was stuck to his foot!

"Yuck!" cried the Invisible Man. "Gum on my toes!"

Wait, his toes? Shouldn't the gum be stuck to the bottom of his shoes?

"And BRRRRR it's cold out here!" he groaned.

Cold? I suppose it was a little chilly. But I felt fine just wearing my T-shirt and jeans.

That's when I realized – Of course! – the Invisible Man wasn't wearing any shoes. Or any clothes at all!

I hadn't thought about it before, but it made total sense. His body was invisible, not his clothes. So if I couldn't see him, that meant he was ... naked. Eww!

I was glad I hadn't realized that when he was chasing me around the Vampire's retirement community! I probably would've been so disgusted that he would have caught me!

But now that I knew, I couldn't let it distract me. I had to focus on escaping him, so I could get back to Bertie before Fran got to him.

As the Invisible Man's invisible hand pulled the gum off of his invisible foot, I ran out of the alley — and then stopped short. On to a busy street! A car whizzed by, just missing me.

Near by, a policeman trotted up on a horse. For a second, I hoped he was coming to help. But he just blew his whistle at me.

"What are you doing running in the middle of the street? Come on, move along!" shouted the policeman. "There's nothing to see here."

"I know," I told him. "That's the problem!"

The Invisible Man could have been anywhere. He could have been in front of me, to the right, or left.

And then suddenly, I felt someone grab my shoulder from behind!

Chapter 6

The hand that had grabbed me spun me around. I saw I was facing an ice cream van.

"JD, is that you?" said the man hanging out of the van's open back door. "What are you doing in the middle of the street in New York City?"

It was Mr Shelley! The head of my orphanage!

I didn't waste any time saying hello or asking Mr Shelley what he was doing here. I jumped into the van, slammed the door behind me and locked it.

MR SHELLEY

"Hey!" roared the other man in the van.

I'd never met him, but I recognized the man immediately. He was Mr Shelley's brother-in-law. He sounded even meaner in person than he did yelling at Mr Shelley over the phone.

Mr Shelley introduced me to his brother-in-law as an orphan from his former orphanage.

"This is the kind of orphan you had at the orphanage?" sneered the brother-in-law as he looked at my mismatched eyes and too-big feet. "No wonder you couldn't find him a family!"

"You're really not very good at anything, are you?" he added. "Besides being married to your sister, I can't think of one good reason why I shouldn't fire you!"

RUDE!

Mr Shelley just hung his head.

After leaving the orphanage, Mr Shelley went to work for his brother-in-law in Las Vegas. He had the idea to drive their ice cream van to New York.

They planned to sell ice cream outside Madison Square Garden, where the Wolves were playing basketball tonight. There wasn't a professional basketball team in Las Vegas. And Mr Shelly thought they were bound to sell more ice cream in a place that had one.

The problem with Mr Shelley's idea was that he wasn't the only one who had had it. There were already lots of other ice cream vans in New York selling ice cream to the fans.

After driving all the way from Las Vegas, Mr Shelley and his brother-in-law hadn't sold any ice cream at all.

Suddenly, someone pounded on the truck.

I didn't look to see who it was. It wouldn't have helped anyway. It had to be the Invisible Man!

"Finally, a customer!" shouted the brother-in-law.

"No, wait!" I cried. The brother-in-law didn't listen.

He stuck his head out of the window.

"Hey, there's no one out here!" he said.

I knew there was someone out there. And it was only a matter of time before he was in here. Unless we got moving.

"We have to go!" I cried.

"We're not going anywhere," roared the brother-in-law. "There was a customer out there a second ago. He might come back."

BOOM! BOOM! BOOM! The

Invisible Man pounded on the side of the truck again.

"You see?" The brother-in-law beamed as he leaned out of the window again. "There he is – Hey! Where'd that customer go?!"

"Right here!" I said.

"What are you talking about?" asked Mr Shelley.

"I'll be your customer!" I said. "I'll buy all the ice cream you've got! Just get me out of here!"

"Yeah, right," snorted the brother-in-law. "How is an orphan going to pay for $514 worth of ice cream?"

"With this!" I said, holding up a few gold coins. The brother-in-law grabbed one and took a bite.

"Tastier than rocky road with coloured sprinkles on top!" he cried. "This'll pay for our whole trip – and then some! You're okay, kid!"

Then he gave Mr Shelley a hug. "And you, too, Shelley! You found us our best customer yet!"

"Good old JD!" beamed Mr Shelley, "You're always there just when I need you!"

Believe me – as we raced away down the street in the ice cream van, leaving the Invisible Man behind – I said the same thing to Mr Shelley!

Chapter 7

Ten minutes later, I was standing outside Bertie's hotel room, holding $514 worth of melting ice cream in my arms.

SO STICKY!

I knew where he was going to be because it was part of his routine. Which meant the Invisible Man and Fran knew too.

I had a head start thanks to the lift Mr Shelley had given me. There was no way the Invisible Man had arrived here before me.

As I pounded on the door, I just hoped Fran was with the Invisible Man – and not already inside with Bertie.

"Oh, it's you," said a very surprised Bertie as he opened the door. "Well, this is unusual."

"Is Fran in there with you?" I asked.

"No," replied Bertie. "I never have visitors at this time. It's not part of my routine. But I do like ice cream. I suppose if I turned you away, I'd have to walk you down to reception. You did bring me ice cream, so that would be the only polite thing to do..."

He shuddered at the thought. "That's simply too much work," he sighed. "So come on in."

I did.

Bertie's hotel room was AMAZING!

It had two bathrooms! And four TVs! Two of which were in the bathrooms! I'd never been in a hotel room with TVs in the bathrooms. Actually, I had never been in a hotel. The whole thing was pretty cool. But I didn't have time to check it all out.

It was only a matter of time before Fran and the IM showed up. I had to get Bertie out of there.

There was just one problem with that: Bertie. He refused to leave his room.

"Go? Oh, I wish you hadn't suggested that," he said as he finished his third ice cream. "Just thinking about it is exhausting. I think I need to lie down."

Bertie flopped down on the bed.

"Ah, yes, much better," he smiled. "I think a good lie down makes almost everything better. Don't you?"

I didn't think so at all. In fact, it seemed like the opposite was true: Bertie's lying down was going to make it that much easier for Fran and the Invisible Man to catch up to us. We had to get out of there.

But not before I had a look at the TV in the bathroom. Okay, I admit it – that was too cool to pass up. I had never been to the toilet while watching TV and, with Fran and the Invisible Man after me, I didn't think I'd get another chance.

Once that was done, we had to get out of there!

I did everything I could to convince him or cajole him or whatever you call it when you try to get someone to do something. But he wouldn't budge.

I knew it wasn't smart to get annoyed, but I couldn't help it. After all I had done, couldn't he do just a little bit?

"Yes, well, that's you, JD," said Bertie, not even making the effort to lift his head off of the pillow to look at me. "Apparently, you enjoy doing things. I don't."

The only thing he wanted to do was the next thing from his daily routine: wait to get today's newspaper delivered.

"Of course, I don't actually read the paper," explained Bertie. "That would take too much effort. But I do like to get the paper every day – the way my father and my grandfather did."

If I wanted to save Bertie's butt, I had to get him out of there. So, thinking fast, I raced out into the corridor. There was the bellboy, marching towards the door, carrying the newspaper.

"Wait! Stop!" I said. "Please, I'm begging you. You've got to tell him you're out of papers and that he has to go out and get one himself."

"Why would I?" asked the bellboy. "If I do that, I won't get a tip."

That made sense to me. "What if I give you this?" I said, handing him one of the Vampire's gold coins.

"Done!" exclaimed the bellboy, marching into Bertie's room. "We're out of newspapers today, Mr Wodehouse. "I'm afraid you'll have to go out and get your own."

And with that, the bellboy turned and left.

"What a bother!" exclaimed Bertie. "Even if I don't read it, I do like to get the paper every day. It's what my father and my grandfather did. And it's part of my routine!"

"You still can," I said. "All we have to do is go out and find a newsagent."

"I don't know," replied Bertie. "That sounds like an awful lot of work."

"Oh, no, it'll be easy," I said.

Luckily, I was wrong.

It wasn't easy at all. We walked for ages. There were no newsagents anywhere we looked. It turned out that no one bought newspapers any more. They all got the news on their phones.

Bertie pulled his jacket and scarf closer around him. "It's a bit chilly out here," he complained as his stomach RUMBLED queasily. "And all this activity definitely does not agree with my digestion. Perhaps we had better go back to the hotel."

"No!" I cried. Fran and the Invisible Man had to be at the hotel by now. We couldn't go back there.

"I mean, no," I said in a calmer voice. "Nowadays, everyone gets the news on their phones. That's what we're going to have to do too."

"But I don't have a phone," Bertie reminded me.

"Then let's go and buy one!" I replied.

"Buy one?" said Bertie with a look of shock. "How?"

"We find a phone shop," I said as patiently as I could. "And then you take out some money or a credit card and pay for a phone."

"Money? A credit card?" he repeated, as if they were foreign words. "I don't have any of those things!"

"You don't?" I said. "Not to be rude, but aren't you pretty rich?"

Bertie thought for a moment. "I think so," he said. "But someone else deals with all of that for me. I just put everything on my bill at the club or the hotel."

"Then I'll buy you a phone," I said, dragging Bertie down the street. "I've still got some more gold coins. If you want to stick to your routine, this is the only way to do it. It'll be easy. I'll take care of everything."

Bertie followed, but he had his doubts.

Which he should have. I didn't know anything about phones. I didn't even have one.

That's why I thought it would take us a long time to buy one when we got to the shop.

I mean, no one wants to help a kid when you go into a shop like that. Everyone's worried you'll break something.

That turned out to be true. Until Bertie mentioned to the salespeople that I had a pocket full of gold coins!

After that, I couldn't get them to stop helping me. They even printed out the selfie Bertie took of the two of us with the phone.

Still, everyone in the shop was so busy showing Bertie all the things the phone could do, it seemed like we would be there for hours.

Until suddenly - **FRRRRRRT!**

"Excuse me," said Bertie as he farted again. "My stomach is not used to all this activity."

After that, it took them less than a minute to take my gold coins and shuffle us out onto the pavement with Bertie's new phone. I couldn't blame them. It smelled as though doing stuff REALLY disagreed with Bertie.

PEWWW!

We stood there on the corner as Bertie played with his new phone. I hoped he would keep doing that all day while Fran and the Invisible Man waited for him back at the hotel.

BEEP! BOOP! Went the phone. BEEP! BEEP! FARRTTT! That last one wasn't the phone. It was Bertie.

I felt bad that making him do stuff was upsetting his stomach. But it was the only way I could think to keep him safe from Fran. And it seemed to be working.

Until a huge car pulled up in front of us. An equally huge driver jumped out and raced right towards Bertie!

"I've come for you," said the driver.

Chapter 8

I leaped between the driver and Bertie.

"Stop!" I cried. "Don't get any closer to him."

But Bertie was already halfway inside the car. I tried to drag him out, but the driver pulled me off him.

"Kid, I'm just trying to do my job here," said the driver.

"Yeah, right – your job kidnapping people for Fran!" I said in the bravest voice I could muster. I put up my dukes or my ducks or whatever you call it when you raise your fists. "How did you track us down?"

"Look, kid, I didn't 'track you down'," said the driver, ignoring my dukes or ducks or whatever you call them. "I'm just trying to get a tip here. The hotel manager sent me straight over after Mr Wodehouse texted him asking for a car."

"Indeed I did!" said Bertie as he opened the door to the back of the car. "Thanks to this new telephone JD here purchased for me!"

Oh, crud!

I had hoped buying a phone would take so long that Bertie would forget about his routine. Instead, all the phone did was enable him to text for a car that would get him right back on schedule!

Wherever he was going to be next, Fran and the Invisible Man were sure to be there waiting for him.

Of course, I tried to tell Bertie that. But Bertie wouldn't listen.

"A ride in this car should do wonders for my stomach," continued Bertie. "Not to mention my legs. I haven't done this much walking around since ... well, I don't think I've ever done this much walking!"

It felt as though my brain was going for a swim inside my head. I didn't know what to do. Until I felt the gold coins in my pocket! I still had a few!

As Bertie settled into the back of the car, I jumped into the front.

"How would you like a really big tip?" I whispered to the driver.

"A lot better than a small one," he admitted.

Five minutes later, Bertie and I were back on the pavement.

"I can't believe the hotel sent us a car that needed an immediate repair," scowled Bertie.

I couldn't believe it either. Because it wasn't true.

I had given the driver three gold coins to lie and say he couldn't take us back to the hotel.

"First the hotel runs out of newspapers, and now this!" said Bertie. "If I didn't find change so exhausting, I might consider moving hotels!"

Bertie looked at his watch. "Speaking of moving," he said. "I have to get to the Rainbow Room for my four p.m. tea!"

Bertie took out his phone to call for another car.

"NO!" I cried. Then I said in a calmer voice, "You said it yourself. The hotel has already messed up twice today. Can we really risk it?"

"You're right." Bertie nodded. "But what else can we do?" he asked.

I looked around, trying to think of an answer. And saw an entrance to the subway.

"We could take the subway," I suggested.

"The subway?" replied Bertie. He had never taken it.

Neither had I. I had no idea how to do it. Probably, it would take a while to work out.

Which was perfect!

Down in the subway station, Bertie and I looked at the map.

"I attended cartography lectures at Princeton," he told me. "That's the study of maps, in case you don't know."

"So what does the map say?" I asked.

"Attending the classes was troublesome enough," Bertie replied. "Actually learning any of it?" He shook his head. "That would have been far too much work."

I had never been to a cartography lecture, but I did have the blood of an explorer (and also his feet). I looked at the map. And immediately saw that the Rainbow Room was only one stop away.

I didn't tell Bertie that. As he couldn't read the map, instead of taking one stop, we'd take ALL the stops.

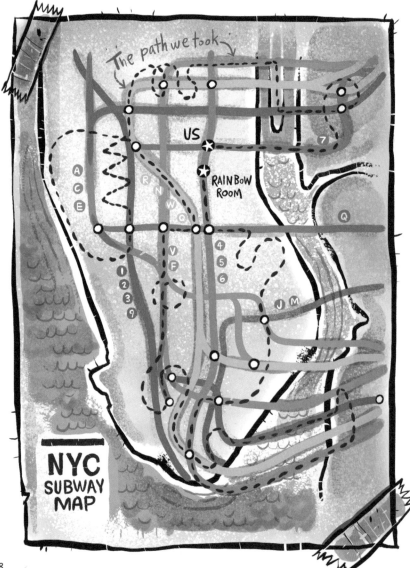

We would have kept going, but all of the activity started to disagree with Bertie and, well, you know ... FRRRRRTTT! The other passengers made us get off at the next stop.

As we crawled out of the subway station just as the sun was setting, Bertie looked at his watch. "We're going to be late for the next part of my routine," he said.

I was glad to hear it.

"That is we would be," he continued. "If the next place I needed to be weren't right here!"

Needless to say, I wasn't as glad to hear that.

The next thing on Bertie's agenda was tea at the Rainbow Room. Which turned out to be at the top of an incredible New York City skyscraper.

the RAINBOW Room

When the lift opened on the top floor, a waitress was there to meet us.

"Welcome back, Bertie," she said.

The waitress led us through the restaurant to the balcony. There were several tables there, sixty-five storeys above Sixth Avenue. Bertie and I sat at one.

As Bertie read the menu, I realized this wasn't going to be a problem. As soon as he ordered, I would just slip away and then use another gold coin to pay the waitress to say they were out of tea.

And we still had time. Looking at the other tables, I didn't see any sign of Fran. I did see the Mummy at one table (it still upset me, what he had done to my town, but I had bigger worries at the moment). At one of the other tables was a group of really tall men.

And – oh, no – the Werewolf!

Chapter 9

If there was anyone in the world who hated me more than Fran and the Invisible Man, it was the Werewolf.

My cousin Sam and I had sent him to prison after – well, that's a whole other story (in fact, it's the story right before the last story in my journal, if you don't remember).

The Werewolf was sitting with the tall men in uniforms. Bertie probably weighed the same as one of them, but he was wider than he was tall. We didn't stand a chance.

The Werewolf raised a paw in the air. And asked a waiter, "May we see some menus?"

That's when I noticed that the uniforms the tall men were wearing all said "Wolves".

The "Werewolf" wasn't the Werewolf at all. He was the mascot for the Wolves basketball team. Phew!

Bertie hadn't even noticed that I was nervous. He'd been busy studying the menu.

I looked over his shoulder and saw that they didn't have any normal food like ham and cheese sandwhiches or fish fingers. I mean, they sort of did. But it was all a bit different.

I suppose that's what made fancy restaurants fancy – they take food you like to eat and then make it slightly strange.

"I don't know why I even bother to look at the menu," Bertie told me. "I always order the same thing: high tea at the highest temperature. In fact, they always bring it to me without having to order."

Okay, all I had to do was give the waitress a gold coin and ask her to tell Bertie the restaurant was out of tea.

I reached into my pocket to pull one out. And came up with nothing but pocket. I was out of coins!

The waitress walked up with the tea. I was doomed.

Even worse, by the time Bertie finished his tea, we'd be finished. Because that would give Fran all the time she needed to get here.

I saw the waitress approach with Bertie's tea. All I could think was, *This really stinks.* That was partly because I don't like the smell of tea. But it was mostly because now that his tea was coming, Bertie wasn't going anywhere. He was going to stick to his routine. After everything I had done today, Bertie was going to sit here until he was finished. I knew there was nothing I could do to change his mind. So I didn't say anything. Bertie didn't say much either. Just two words to the waitress who held his tea: "No thanks."

"But isn't this what you always order?" replied the confused waitress. "Is there something wrong?"

"There's nothing wrong at all!" said Bertie with a smile. "Quite the opposite, in fact! I've had a delightful day doing things for myself. Have you ever tried it? It's really quite interesting!"

The waitress assured Bertie that she'd done many things for herself. Several that very day, in fact.

"Then you know all about it," exclaimed Bertie. "I'm just learning. I had no idea it could be so invigorating. Not great for the stomach," he admitted. "But wonderful for the mind!"

Then Bertie did something even more shocking. He got up! Out of his chair!

"Let's go and get our own tea, JD. I'm sure we can find some in a..." he paused for a moment. "What do you call those places that sell foodstuffs?" he asked.

"A supermarket?" I replied.

"Yes, that's what I'm talking about!" he exclaimed. "I've been driven past them before. Never been inside. A supermarket. Sounds exciting! Like a place where a superhero would have an adventure!"

I couldn't imagine any hero having an adventure in a supermarket. But that was okay. I didn't want excitement. I wanted the opposite. Anywhere that wasn't part of Bertie's usual routine would be safe and quiet. A supermarket was as good a place as any.

I relaxed for the first time in hours. All my problems were solved! Including the problem of having no more gold coins. As Bertie had turned away his tea without tasting it, we didn't even have to pay for it.

Yep, it definitely looked like my luck was changing, as I looked over from our table at the lift. DING! The doors slid open. Perfect timing! One passenger stepped out.

Unfortunately, it was Fran.

OH NUTS!

Chapter 10

As Fran walked through the restaurant, tables flew up in the air behind her.

Of course, I knew it was the Invisible Man knocking them over. But no one else did. They panicked.

Except the Wolf mascot and the Wolves. They got everyone else to the stairs and out of the restaurant.

By the time Fran reached us on the balcony, Bertie and I were all alone.

"Hello there, Fran," he said. "We were just leaving."

"No, you're leaving with me," she replied. "And I doubt JD is leaving here at all."

"Isn't that right?" she said to no one at all.

"Yeah," grunted the Invisible Man.

I heard him rush at me. I was right up against the edge of the balcony. There was nowhere to run. I looked around for something – anything! – I could use to stop him. All I saw was the tea the waitress had brought for Bertie.

The super-high-temperature tea!

As I heard the Invisible Man charge at me, I poured the tea all over the floor. His invisible – and bare! – feet hit the super-hot tea.

It didn't bother me, Bertie or Fran. Because we were wearing shoes. But it burned the Invisible Man's bare feet!

"Yow!! Ow!! Ow!!" he cried as he jumped around in pain. But the hot tea was everywhere. He leaped up, only to splash down in more hot tea. "Yow!" he cried as he hopped up again – right over the balcony railing!

"Ahhhhhhhhh!" he cried as he fell. I couldn't see if he smashed down to the ground or stopped his fall somehow. He was invisible, after all.

But I had bigger worries. Because as the Invisible Man fell over the railing, he pushed me over too!

I tumbled over the side of the balcony. It reminded me of the time I jumped out of the plane over Antarctica. Only I was a lot higher up now.

And instead of soft snow there was nothing but concrete below!

Suddenly, a rope fell down alongside me. I grabbed it. It was slimy. And it smelled like it hadn't been washed in a thousand years.

It hadn't. Because this was no rope. It was the Mummy's bandage!

No matter how bad the Mummy's bandage smelled, I had to admit this mummy didn't stink! He was okay in my book. Now I just had to survive long enough to write that down in my book!

The Mummy had unwound most of himself to save me. He couldn't do anything else. Neither could I until I climbed back up.

Bertie was up there with Fran, and there was no one who could help. It was up to Bertie to do something to save himself. Which meant he was doomed.

Fran moved closer to him.

"Bertie," I shouted from below. "Don't just stand there. Do something!"

"'Do something?'" he replied. "You make that sound so easy."

"What should I do? I'm not used to having to come up with things to do!"

"Don't worry," said Fran. "You'll never have to do anything again. You won't be able to escape me this time. Not when I have this!"

She held up her phone.

"It's my brand-new invention," she said proudly. "I call it ... the Cell Phone!"

"Um, I don't mean to burst your bubble," said Bertie. "But the cell phone isn't exactly a new invention. I've even got one. Thanks to JD."

He held up his phone.

"That's a cell phone," sneered Fran. "Mine may look like that from the outside, but I've completely rewired it from the inside to turn it into a Cell Phone that will trap you in an impenetrable cell!"

Fran turned on her Cell Phone and pushed buttons.

VRRRUM! Her Cell Phone started warming up.

I was hanging a few metres below them. I couldn't get to Bertie in time. But then I realized that maybe there were other people who could. Police. The fire service. Bertie had his phone in his hand. All he had to do was call them!

"Bertie," I cried. "Your phone! Use it!"

"I thought about that," he said. "But it seemed like an awful lot of work and –"

"Do it!!!" I cried.

"Okay," said Bertie.

He held up his phone and ... threw it at Fran. It wasn't much of a throw. The phone landed about a metre away from Fran.

"Ah well," sighed Bertie as he slumped down in a comfy chair. "I tried."

"No!" I cried as I climbed up the smelly bandage.

"You didn't! You could still do a lot more!"

"You could," replied Bertie. "Not me. I'm sorry, JD, but I'm just not like you. I think it would just be easier if I let her take me."

"So do I!" agreed Fran as she aimed her Cell Phone at Bertie.

I couldn't believe it. After everything I had done, he wouldn't even get off his butt to save himself. I climbed as fast as I could, but it wasn't fast enough.

All I could do was watch as ... FRRRRRTTT! Bertie let out the biggest fart yet! Which meant I could do more than watch – I could smell it too!

So could Fran! It was pretty powerful stuff. She stumbled.

And dropped her Cell Phone. Just as it went off! FRZAAAP! A beam of light shot out of it. And hit Fran! She was trapped.

Yikes! Bertie wouldn't get off his butt to save himself – but then his butt saved him!

The police arrived a little while later, alerted by the Wolves and the rest of the people who had fled the Rainbow Room.

Still trapped by her Cell Phone, Fran was taken away.

Having finally climbed up onto the balcony, I thanked the Mummy. Whatever he had done to my hometown, we were even. And I would make sure everyone back at home knew it.

"GRRRRN," replied the Mummy.

Bertie rushed up and gave me a hug.

"We have more in common than I thought!" he exclaimed. "Did you see what I did?"

I had. Well, actually, I had mostly just smelled it. But still. I couldn't have been prouder.

"You did it, Bertie!" I exclaimed. "All by yourself!"

"Well, I did have some help from my posterior," he replied. "But that makes sense. That is how I am related to you, after all."

As the police swarmed around, I whispered to Bertie that I had to go. I had learned from past experience that if I got involved with the police, I would have to spend days and days with them. And I couldn't afford to waste that time.

Bertie was safe from Fran for now. But if I knew Fran Kenstein, she would find a way to cause more trouble for my cousins.

I had to find them and warn them first.

As Bertie proudly told the police what he had done ("You'll never believe what I did today," he told them. "I took the subway!"), I tapped my email address into Bertie's phone and then slipped out the back.

About a week later, I got this message:

From: BertramIV@

Subject: FWD: Letter of Recommendation

Dear JD

Hope you don't mind, but I went ahead and wrote a letter to my friend the Dean about you. I know you won't be thinking about which university you want to go to for a few years, but when you do, I hope you will consider Princeton. You'd have a very good chance of getting in. You're smart, resourceful and you're obviously a hard worker. But you've got something that's even more important to have when applying to Princeton: family who went there! It means a lot to the admissions officers, I can assure you. That's what got me in!

Your cousin,
Bertie

Begin forwarded message:
From: BertramIV@
To: AdmissionsDean@

Dear Dean,

I'm writing to recommend a young man for admission to Princeton: my cousin, JD. He's got a few years to go, but when he is ready he is exactly the kind of student the University needs. Not only would he learn a lot at Princeton, but everyone would learn a lot from him. I know I did! Such as how to ride the subway (Have you ever tried it? It's very interesting!). And even more, he taught me to get off my butt and do things for myself, which – no offence to my former professors – is the most important lesson I have ever learned.

Thank you for your consideration,

Bertram Wodehouse IV

GLOSSARY

associate fellow worker, colleague, friend or partner

cartography art of making maps

cell phone mobile phone

impenetrable impossible to get through

orphanage place where children who don't have parents live and are looked after

posterior rear end of the body, particularly the bottom or butt

revenge action of hurting or harming someone in return for an injury or wrong caused by them

subway underground railway found in cities

NOT AS SCARY AS HE LOOKS!

Scott Sonneborn has written several books, one script for a circus performance (for Ringling Bros. and Barnum & Bailey) and many TV series. He's been nominated for one Emmy award and spent three very cool years working at DC Comics. He lives in California, USA, with his wife and their two sons.

COOLEST ILLUSTRATOR EVER!

Timothy Banks is an award-winning illustrator known for his ability to create magically quirky illustrations for children and adults. He has a Master of Fine Arts degree in Illustration, and he also teaches art students in his spare time. Timothy lives in South Carolina, USA, with his wonderful wife, two beautiful daughters and two crazy pugs.